Rumpelstiltskin

ILLUSTRATED BY STEPHE

Story adapted by
Christine Deverell

D1443971

Once there was a poor miller who had a very beautiful daughter. He was so poor, he couldn't pay his taxes, and when the King threatened to put him in prison, the miller in desperation said, "I have a daughter who can spin gold out of straw."

"Then bring her to me immediately," ordered the King.

The frightened girl was led to a room which was filled with a huge pile of straw.

"Spin all this into gold before morning, or you will be punished," ordered the King. The miller's daughter pleaded to be excused, for she knew that she was not able to spin gold out of straw, but it was no use. The door was locked and she sat there alone and wept.

After a while, the door opened and in walked a little man. "Why are you sad?" he asked.

"The King has ordered me to spin all this straw into gold, and I don't know how to do it."

"What will you give me if I do it for you?" said the

little man. The girl gave him her necklace, and he sat down

to work, spinning the straw into fine gold. By morning he was finished.

The King was delighted with what he saw, but he wanted more. So he took the miller's daughter to a larger room filled with straw and told her to spin it into gold by the next morning. Again she sat down and wept.

Soon, the little man came into the room and said, "What will you give me if I do this for you?" She gave him her gold ring, and he worked until morning, when the task was complete.

The King was greedy and wanted even more gold, so

the next evening he took the girl to an even larger room,

filled to the rafters with straw. He said, "If you do this

tonight, you will be my wife."

The little man came in as before and asked her, "What

will you give me to spin all this into gold for you?"

She despaired, for she had nothing left to give him.

"Then promise me," said the little man, "your first child

when you are queen."

The miller's daughter could only

agree to give the little

man what he

wanted though she hoped that she would never have to keep her promise.

Once again the peculiar little man spun a huge pile of gold, and not a piece of straw was left.

In the morning the King found all he wanted, and the miller's daughter became his Queen.

A year passed, and the Queen gave birth to a lovely daughter. She was so happy that she forgot about the funny little man and the promise she made, until one day he appeared and reminded her of it. She offered him all the treasure of the kingdom but he

refused to accept it. She cried and cried because she could

not bear to part with her little baby.

The little man gave in to her pleading saying, "Very well, I will give you three days, and if in that time you can guess my name, then you may keep your child." The Queen stayed up all night thinking of all the names she had ever heard and writing them down in a long list.

The next day, the little man came to her room and she began to work through the list. Peter, John, Mark, Isaac, Thomas, Henry, Jeremiah . . . But with every name she tried she received the same reply: "No! That's not my name."

On the second day she tried all the strangest names that she had heard of, and some that she made up herself, like Roofabeef, Gug and Boogie. But the little man just laughed and said, "You will never guess my name!" The Queen sent her servants out to see if they could discover any other names.

All but one returned with no new names. But late in the evening, as the remaining servant was making his way

back to the castle, he heard a little man singing in the woods:

"Merrily the feast I'll make,

Today I'll brew, tomorrow bake;

Merrily I'll dance and sing,

For next day a stranger bring:

Little does my lady dream

Rumpelstiltskin is my name!"

This faithful servant told the Queen of his fortunate discovery, and when on the third day her little visitor arrived, she asked him,

"Is your name William?" "No."

"Is it Charles?" "No."

"Could it be . . . Rumpelstiltskin?"

"Who told you that? Who told you that?" cried the little man; and he shook his fists and stamped his feet so hard that he made a hole in

20

the floor and fell right into it.

Moaning and groaning, he pulled himself out of the hole and ran away. The Queen lived happily with the King and her daughter, and they were never bothered by Rumpelstiltskin again.